Amma's Tales

PRESENTS

Tail Tales

VOLUME I

STORIES BY HEMA VAIDYANATHAN

ILLUSTRATED BY KISHORE MOHAN & COLOURED BY ROSHAN

Once upon a time, in the kingdom of Ayodhya, there lived a prince called Rama. The seventh avatar of Lord Vishnu, Rama was loved by his people.

Because of his father's promise to his step-mother, Kaikeyi, Rama, along with his wife, Sita, and brother, Lakshmana, was sent to live in the forests for fourteen years. Their life was changed forever when the ten-headed king of Lanka, Ravana, kidnapped Sita.

With the help of the monkey king, Sugriva, and his monkey army, Rama marched to Lanka. Crossing forests, climbing mountains and, finally, bridging the ocean, Rama destroyed Ravana and rescued Sita.

This is the story of the Ramayana that we know and love so well. Sugriva and Hanuman helped Rama win his battle. But there are the forgotten heroes – brave and strong kings, small and tiny animals - without whose help Sita may never have been rescued.

Here are some of their stories…

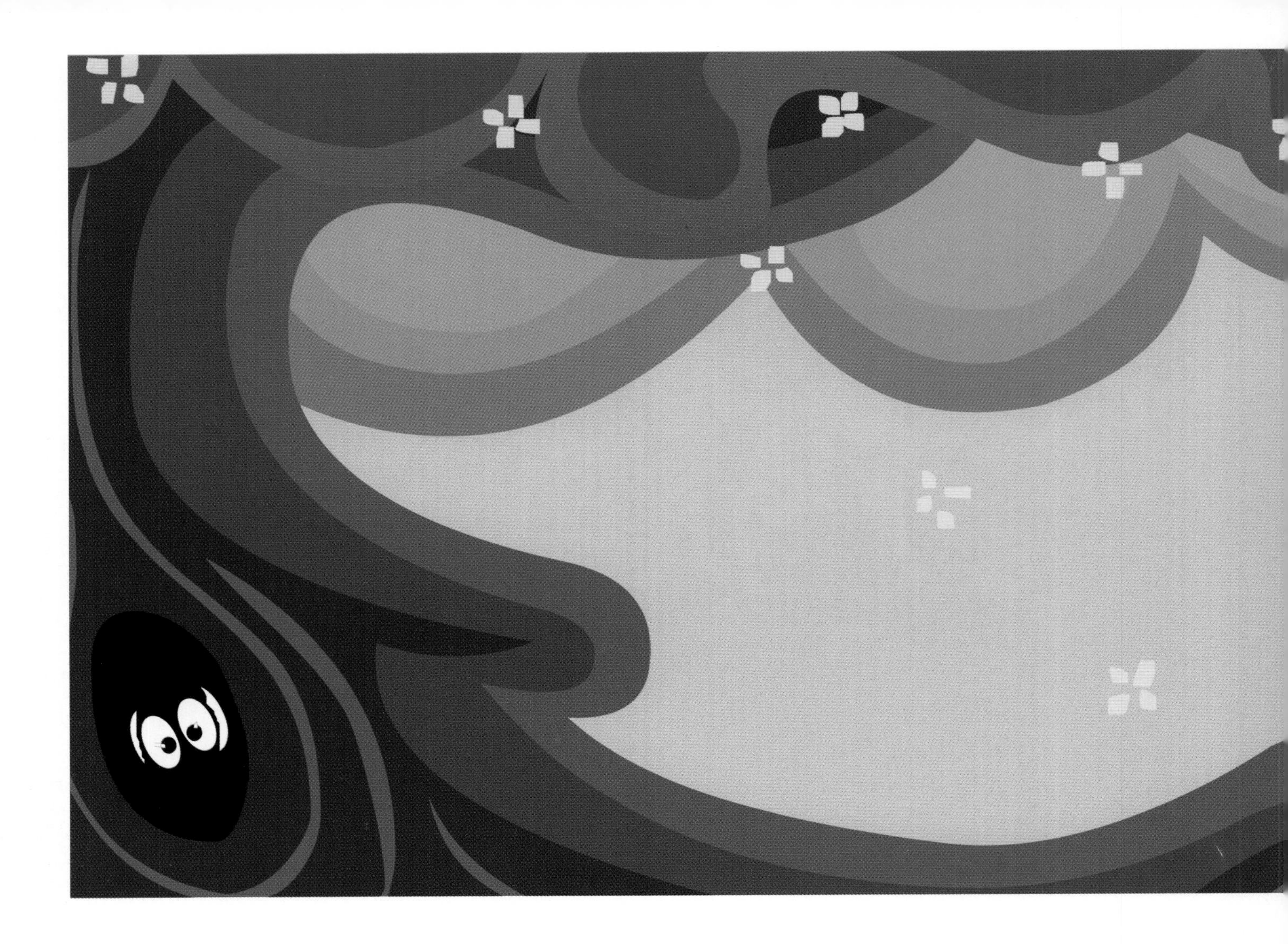

A Powerful Tail

Vali was the monkey-king of Kishkindha and all was well in his world. He had a beautiful wife, Tara, and a baby son, Angada. "Ah!" thought Vali. "My people are prosperous, food is aplenty and I am content."

But the peace didn't last for long. One day, Vali had to defend his kingdom from the invading armies of the neighbouring monkey-king. In the fierce battle that followed, Vali's tail was cut off.

Vali was very upset. "My people will laugh at me. Whoever heard of a monkey-king without a tail? I had better disappear before someone sees me like this." Ashamed, Vali slunk away from the battlefield under the cover of darkness.

"At least the battle was won," he comforted himself. "I did not desert my men and watch them lose as well. I hope Sugriva has the sense to guide them all back to Kishkindha."

Meanwhile, Vali's victorious army marched back to Kishkindha without their king. Leading the army back home, Sugriva wondered, "Where *is* Vali? We've been waiting so long for him and he hasn't shown up yet. I don't want the men to think their king is lost. I hope he's back in Kishkindha already."

But Vali was heading off in the opposite direction– into the deepest depths of the forests near Kishkindha. The loss of his tail was bothering Vali.

"What am I going to do?" he thought. "Lizards grow back their tails easily... but I'm a monkey! What *am* I going to do? There has got to be a way!"

Staring sadly at the little stump of tail that was left behind, Vali decided to pray. Concentrating all his thoughts upon Shiva, Vali prayed like he had never prayed before. Finally, Shiva appeared before him. "Vali," said Shiva. "Rise! I am pleased with you. What is it that you want?"

Suddenly feeling foolish for what he was asking, Vali mumbled, "O Shiva, I only want one thing... and that is for my tail to grow back. Can you do that?"

Shiva laughed, “Is that all, Vali? No special powers, no amazing riches, no fantastic muscles? Just a tail?” Even more embarrassed that Shiva was teasing him now, Vali said, “Just a tail. As a king I must have the respect of my people. And so, as a *monkey*-king, I must have a tail!”

Shiva was impressed by Vali’s humility. He said, “Vali, you have shown yourself to be a true leader. Even when you had a chance to ask for anything you wanted from the gods, you chose the one thing that you knew would help everyone around you– a safe kingdom in the hands of a good king.”

Shiva bent to touch the remaining little bit of Vali’s tail and it began to grow, long and magnificent.

Shiva said, “Vali, your tail has been blessed by me. It is now your strongest weapon and has unmatched power. Your enemies will never be able to escape from it. Go back to Kishkindha now. Your people are waiting for you!”

Happy with the great power given to his beautiful new tail, Vali ran back to Kishkindha. All the vanaras celebrated the return of their king.

Vali’s tail, blessed by Shiva himself, quickly became his greatest weapon. Any enemy caught in its twisted embrace was easily crushed.

Floating Stones

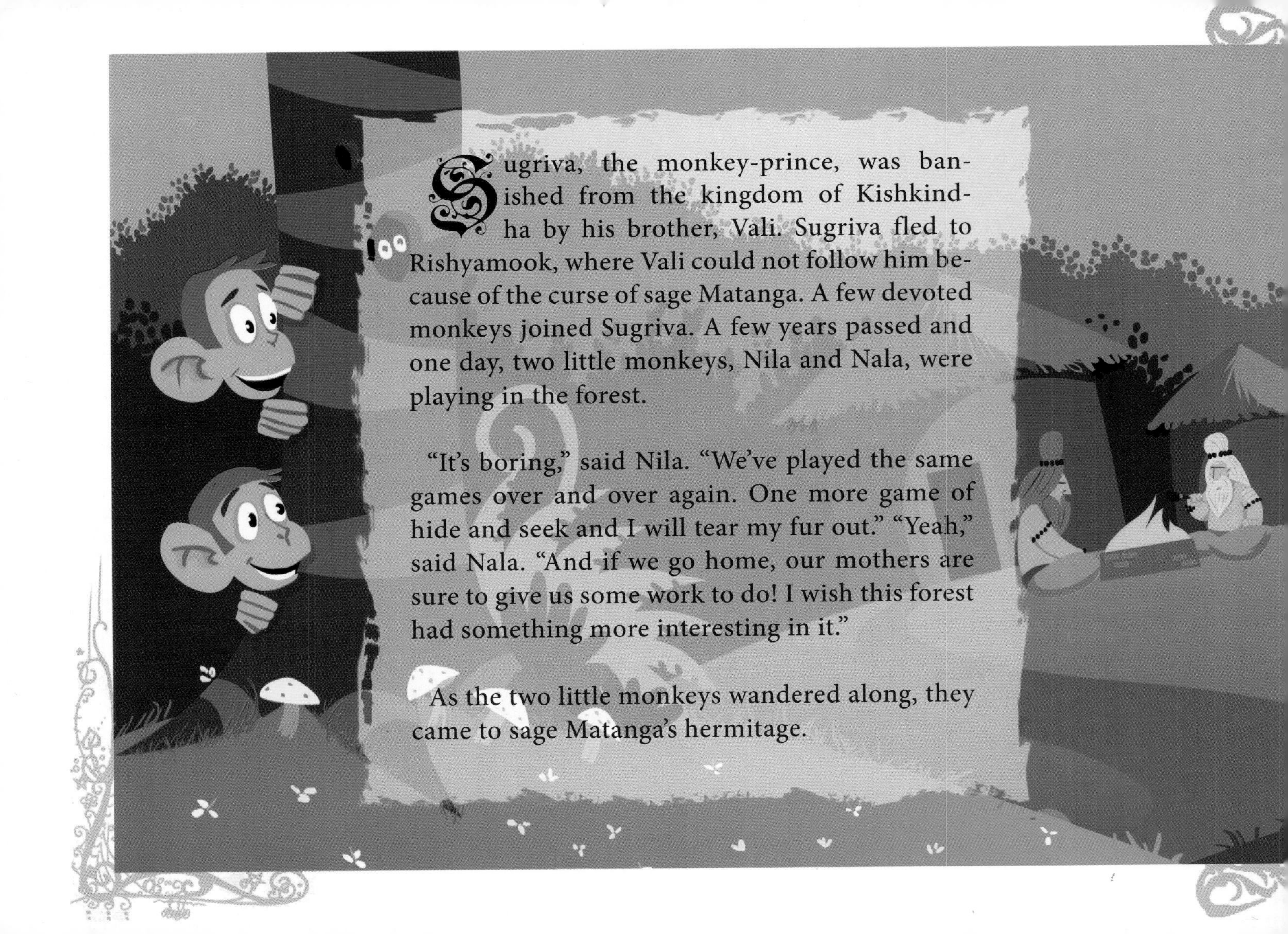

Sugriva, the monkey-prince, was banished from the kingdom of Kishkindha by his brother, Vali. Sugriva fled to Rishyamook, where Vali could not follow him because of the curse of sage Matanga. A few devoted monkeys joined Sugriva. A few years passed and one day, two little monkeys, Nila and Nala, were playing in the forest.

"It's boring," said Nila. "We've played the same games over and over again. One more game of hide and seek and I will tear my fur out." "Yeah," said Nala. "And if we go home, our mothers are sure to give us some work to do! I wish this forest had something more interesting in it."

As the two little monkeys wandered along, they came to sage Matanga's hermitage.

Preparations were on for a big ceremony. Water was being brought, the courtyard was being washed, children were being scrubbed. At the centre of it all, Sage Matanga was setting up the sacred fire.

"I have an idea!" said Nila. Let's go and take some of the stuff they have and drop it in the well. That should give them something to be mad about!" "Hehehe! What fun!" said Nala. "Let's do it!"

Mounds of fruits, flowers and sweets had been set out in front of the fire. Nila and Nala jumped down, grabbed some fruits and flowers and dashed away. The rishis first stared and then quickly tried to chase them.

Nala and Nila went to the well and threw the fruits and flowers into it. Chattering with laughter at the angry faces of everyone in the ashram, the monkeys got too clever. They grabbed even more things from around the fire and tossed them into the well.

Sage Matanga had had enough. He raised his hand and, pointing at the two monkeys, he said, "Stop!" The two monkeys found that they were frozen in mid-air.

The whole ashram started laughing at the plight of the two tiny monkeys who, only moments before, had been causing such havoc!

"Wh...what's happening, Nila?" blubbered Nala. "I can't move, and those rishis look a little angry! What should we do?"

Thinking quickly, Nila said, "O rishis, please forgive us. We are just tiny monkeys. We were bored and trying to have some fun. Please let us go."

Matanga said, "All right, monkeys. You may have learnt your lesson but you need a little punishment. From this day forth, whatever you two throw into water will not sink but will stay afloat." He released the two monkeys from his spell and Nala and Nila gratefully bounded away.

Nila and Nala spent the rest of their summer trying very hard to make stones sink in water. Their ability to make things float had a use for Rama. Sugriva sent his monkey army, including Nala and Nila, to help Rama.

When they reached the ocean, Nila and Nala tossed boulders into the water. Their special talent kept the large stones floating and bridged the ocean between the mainland and Lanka.

amma's Learning corner

spot these words:

Slunk
Fantastic
Plight
Hermitage
Magnificent
Invading

amma asks:

Who did Vali pray to so that his tail would grow back?

What did Nila and Nala do to anger the sages?

Did you know...

Vali was so strong, Sugriva was scared to fight with him. So when Rama offered to help, Sugriva asked Rama to hide behind a tree and shoot Vali!

Glossary

Avatar: Incarnation of Lord Vishnu upon the Earth. He came in nine avatars to rid the world of evil. We're waiting for the tenth!

Kishkindha: Vali's kingdom, populated entirely by monkeys who loved their brave king!

Ashram: Home of sages in the forest, where they stayed with their family and students and meditated.

Angada: Vali's son, he grew up to be a powerful warrior and was a major general in the battle against Ravana.

Indra: The king of the gods. He is the ruler of the heavens and famed for his courage and use of weapons.

spot three differences between the two pictures: